THE DREAD OF INIQUITY CHRISTMAS (ENGLISH)

LE ENDLESS RECESS OF RATHORE BARELY

SUMEET KUMAR

Sumeet Kumar

Sumeet Kumar , A adult who experiences many phases of love in his life , get broked many times , stands up every time and keep moving to the next phases of the life.In reality he is a writter as well as singer (as a hobby).

Very exciting and interesting fact about him is that he is aauthor of New era i.e. he starts his journey of writing at the age when he was going to schools to get the study.His some famous works i.e. Maturity Of Love (Genre - Love),Privacy For Dream (Genre - Middle Class), Army Squad ofLove (Genre- The Seperation of Army Love), 5 Days of Love(Genre- Temporarily Love), Th e Endearment Of Love(Genre - Historical Era Of Love), Social Destruction Indo-Pak (Genre - The Story of The Love At The Time Of Division Of India And Pakistan), Middle Class Soul (Genre - The Dreams of Middle Class), The Accursed Kanatpur (Genre -The Horrific Story Of A Village), Wrong Number (Genre -The Suspenseful Physco Killer Story), The Secrecy OfDeadly Midnight (Genre - The Suspense About a Crime),Fragile Religious Of Death (Genre- The Death Of A TrustfulPerson), Nature Vs Science (Genre - The Future Battle Between Nature And Science In A Horrific Way), Generic Man (Genre - The Dream of I.I.T), The Unconsious 12 Hours(Genre - The Illusion At Stage Of Comma), The StrangeBurden (Genre - The Burden Of Love) , Her Existence (Genre- The Female Pain In The Society) , Jockstrap Prize (Genre -The True Story Of A National Athlete) , H Man [Hindi] (Genre - Superhero Tragic Story), H Man [English] (Genre - Superhero Tragic Story) , Maturity Of Love [Englsih] (Genre - Love) and many more are available on various geners on the offcial platform of **Amazon, Flipkart and Notionpress**. You can buy them from there.

Contents

PREFACE

Christmas Day

Christmas is a festival of the Christian faith that marks the birth of Jesus Christ, the son of God. It is one of the widely celebrated global festivals. It is celebrated on the 25th of December by billions of people. It is celebrated by both Christians and non-Christians as a cultural festival and is central to the holiday season that comes by in December. It marks a season of happiness, joy and sharing.

The history behind Christmas goes the gospels of Luke and Mathew which describe the story of the Birth of Jesus Christ. He was born in Bethlehem and is proclaimed to be the saviour of all people. The scene of his birth also known as the Nativity is recreated using figurines in many households and places of worship. This is one of the important religious symbols associated with Christmas.

The other Christmas traditions include the Christmas tree, exchanging presents and so on. Houses are decorated in beautiful colours of red, white and green using wreaths, Christmas trees, lights and stars. The Christmas tree is decorated with various ornaments such as bells, stars and lights. These are elements of excitement associated with Christmas.

The legend of the Santa Claus is a tradition associated with Christmas. The Santa Claus is said to bring presents for children that are made using the help of his elves.

People dress up as Santa Claus to distribute gifts to children. Exchange of gifts around the Christmas is a way of bringing in joy and expresses the spirit of sharing. Music carols and church sermons are other religious traditions associated with Christmas.

Christmas is a widely celebrated festival across the world. The arte several elements and traditions of happiness associated with it. It comes along with a spirit of happiness that us gives the entire season. It is an occasion for families to get together. Keeping up the spirits of the season by spreading through charity and helping other can be another innovative tradition that we could all include into our Christmas.

But this story tells the mystery of a family who went for holiday at the day before christmas on a unknown place for which they have to pay a very high price by making their life in danger. So , the family try to survive there and there is a huge mystery on the **CHRISTMAS DAY**. So, read the story and understand the mystery with suspense.

Acknowledgements

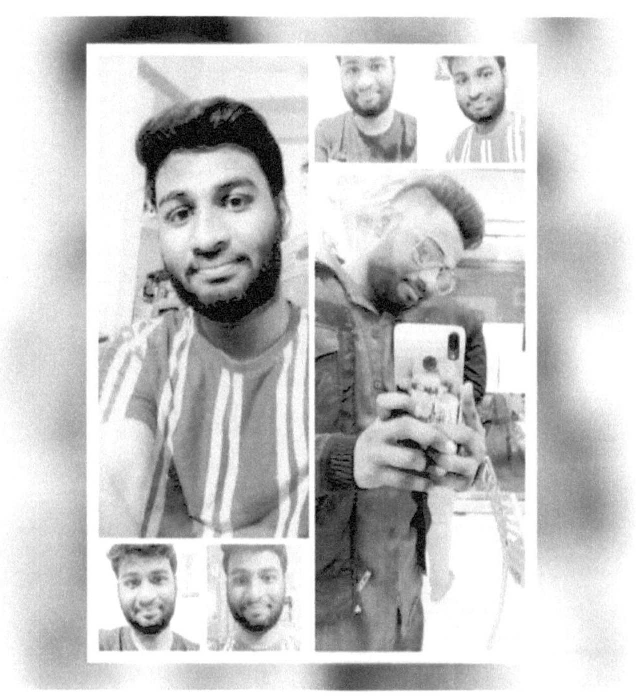

AMAN KUMAR

Special Thanks to **Aman Kumar** who worked so hard in the preparation of this book. He has continually put with my passive voice, omission of words, and late night calls. You have be en wonderful. Thanks to him for his precious time in reviewing proposals , individual chapters and early drafts, along with his suggestions on the applicability of the material to the world.

I

The Deaf Truth

It is said that even if a person's body goes away from him, his feet never get away from him, a good anger and a bad anger are seen from both sides, it is quite different, even today, the feet talk to each other, which is of happiness. Be good, human beings change, their feet never change, because their passion starts with loyalty and loyalty ends with the feet, why should humanity bear bow down in front of someone and never leave one's own fear. Whatever wrong we do in the world, we get punishment one day and no witness in the world can turn away from the teachings because somewhere or the other, he has also suffered this, the condition of time never changes, all these things to say if time And if the situation starts changing, it may also happen that the person's nature may also change, then it is not because it is never going to happen, life is not what we get, we try to live it in a better way. Maybe that person can be in the society, whose love comes from love, not love, and only that person can love in the world. No matter where humanity is alive, the whole life goes out to handle our pain, which we get due to the breakdown of our dreams, it is in the love of someone with whom we are very much in love and he leaves us when we have to leave him.

The most important thing is that there is no limit to a person's life, because if he had, he would not have the love to live, a time comes in the life of all of us, when we get angry with ourselves, there is such a way to hurt ourselves. Journey goes on feet, where we meet only people who are like us, feet never understand our pain better than us The reason goes on because if this is not included in life, then relationships also seem like a kind of banal at times. Those who care about time, those who care about themselves and those who do not care about themselves, only those walls of pain always silence them It always hurts itself. The grave is such a power of the world where a witness gets two moments of peace. They say that if he says then he can make his life longer, even God does not say that he should be there now because it is said that a good person dies very soon and a bad person does not die soon, I do not say this. Keep in mind that they should not live in the world of education, because since childhood, everyone is not bad, feet are sorry in the heart that why good people leave that too soon from the world .

> *"Pains Recommended*
> *nights Long live Live as much work as you*
> *want"*

In the world of education, any witness is bad when his thinking is bad because man has not created thinking, thinking has made man and it can be called many logs wrong. Will not pass, love is a race with someone's male foot, where we can not even imagine that the nights that were cut in someone's infidelity can give birth to the only witness who has ever supported someone in every difficulty, the world logs a lot of work Those who say to live their life always with each other, a lot of work is logged, who also have the desire to ruin themselves in the love of good reputation, feet can testify such love, who has told someone else more than himself. care about someone else's own family, mind and world too.

> *"In love, even if you are separated from me,*
> *I have left myself behind in the same way."*

Logs are born with a face these days, the enmity behind it is always more than a face, which we often know by the name of the mouth, that everyone in the world is doomed, everyone has to himself. Leaving us to love someone else, say that no other person should do it, yet we will make our home in the festival of happiness, whose walls also take pride in seeing us, there is no fault of theirs in this and after all, because they Toh is never wrong, it is not wrong, Toh we who call us the pride of the festival, who has rejected us since when and has made someone else's right, a real thing, in life, someone can be with you in the journey of life. Absolutely not in a bad condition because in a bad condition, he leaves himself with him, so what will you complain about to another who was never yours, the evidence about which I am going to reveal in the school, he may have loved like that. Forgetting one's own bitterness, don't touch it for someone else. Friendship is such a thing that we are the best in the world. It seems to be one of the things, I mean it seems to be one of the relationships, even if we break up, then the second has the courage that keeps us together You will never be able to play it, you will be able to spend two moments of peace with him because I do not think so and when your own family is not with you for a long time, will you ever live because the feeling of happiness is not even called death.

"What do we complain about when we call our own waste our own waste?"

Death is not a better thing, when a foot is found, it is a comfort because no one can ruin the margin behind which the mouths of enmity are attached, because they give their own humanity in the middle of a great gathering where so many buyers are involved. That we can't do anything even thinking about them. Heart breaking is considered a good training in bad log gatherings in the world because they always get the passion to play it only from someone's breath. If you are telling me, first write the fate of your own ruin in a paper because there is no one to support you in this very special gathering, if any witness shows you sympathy even for a moment, then go to the society at the very first time. He is going to give you such a pain, about which you would never have thought of. Where everyone only hates us, these people think only those logs who are good at heart, if feet are better than good people When the world goes on, he himself never calls his servant to himself. The gathering seems deserted only when someone's pain is recommended because before that everyone prepares for their celebration. It is only by money that if someone in the world plays his relationship honestly, then he does it only with money because if you have a profession in the world then you can also buy relationships, but they will support you only till your Have a profession, in the world, we have become very distant from the word of humanity because no one can bear the pain of anyone, everyone wants their own happiness and nothing else, what is needed that they make your pain their pain. Help you, may it ever worry you, one thing should always be understood by a person, just like past and future can never be one, like love and deceit can never live inside a wall. It is given where we have to say to ruin someone else's gathering to keep ourselves safe, what is the use if someone Keep yourself safe too and your humanity will also get a little more chance to live even at a happy time When he needs someone and that need is in reality trust, if you trust someone more than yourself then you are the most stupid person in the world because the trust which you have given to someone else is actually a good thing. It is not only because he wants your love, that too in his own luck and not in your destiny, so if you have to ask for love in the world, then you will not find anyone better than yourself, then learn to love yourself, sir. And if it is said, then you should also learn to give pain to your own nafs, well, whatever things I should not say, in the end I am saying this, so this story is of a house whose walls were also named after happiness. Whe was buried, every silence of her was related to some or the other silence, whose voice in the room was also she herself, the story of her pain Was attached to the friends of Bishush at a time when no one else was with him in his past, but his own anger was with him.

> **"Humans were not wrong.**
> **I realized this.**
> **Everyone greeted me after my death."**

Well, if we ask you to tell the education of Alfazo, then we will get away from the story of Ruth, who had neither any love nor any friendship nor any true relationship in her gathering and she was well aware of everything. too, he chose male pain because he felt that love was always one step ahead of someone's hatred.

II
Heal The Pain

There are some pains in the world which cannot be eradicated because only one can give that pain and every witness in the world will surely know that there is never any medicine for the pain given to oneself. Not even that the relationships which are of blood, they are called relationships in reality, because nowadays even if someone is alien, we feel like our own, we collide with a new thinking every day, we meet new logs, we share with new logos, sometimes feet themselves Have you ever thought of doing things? Have you ever given yourself the time that you give to someone else, because your self-esteem never looks at us with hatred, nor does it involve us in any enmity. Where would I have to ask a question to all of them that after all logs are not bad, then what is the angle of evil in the world, what is their thinking, this is their humanity, which is included in the four walls of the world with a new face every day. After all, who is the culprit, can anyone tell me whose thinking is that which would have compelled us so much that we would have started hating someone else? What is the benefit of such a disease that makes you an animal, when our head burns in the world, then our anger stays with us at the same time, neither our effort nor our thinking is this farg. In the story of which you all have to I am going to tell that witness is none other than Adrika Rathore, a girl who said someone else than herself, she had seen someone else's happiness before her own happiness, that girl was not weak, her feet made her weak because of her love. The love that has never been in his mind, even if he has ever been infatuated with his body, it is not because of him, the love in which the body is talked about is only a deception and nothing else, the feet are some logs which kill the poison. Let's also assume that Adrika had no shortage of anything, feet say that if she has education for everything, then God always keeps away from one thing, which we call love only, God can achieve everything in the world. May be someone's faith and someone's true love is found only by luck, this is not a market education which should be distributed among everyone. We all have to be aware of one thing of the truth, because what I am going to tell in reality, probably everyone will know the evidence, if some logs believe it, then nothing but the good logs in the world are leaving us very soon. The walking feet that are bad, they never take the name of going away from us, we keep walking through the story where Adrika's anger is still imprisoned Adrika was the daughter of a very big house, I mean her father's She had a lot of profession and she was also their only daughter. Adrika's mother had died in her childhood, that too in an accident where her father was also present, at that time she did not even break her feet.

Rathore sir's luck is very good because the feet survived the accident by doing so big, there is also a mystery behind it which you all may come to know later, because its streak is also related to happiness, so many pains are right even in someone's love. And from her family too, when Adrika's mother died, Adrika would probably be 10 years old when her mother died. He is behind the death, so when she was 15 years old, she left her home where she lived and after that she came to Bangalore and started living with her aunt, where her mother was not there, her aunt Maria Emmanuel gave her He was brought up with great love because he had no one of his own, so he used to love his friend's daughter Adrika very much, he never let her feel that her mother is no longer in the world, whenever she remembers even a little. John Maria never let him feel the silence, she was with him all the time and supported him all the time, a lot of work is logged in the world One who takes someone else's pain as her own pain and becomes a participant in their pain, removes all their pain. When Aadrika lived with her Aunt Maria, she may have forgotten that she has someone in the world who is still alive. I mean, Log used to say to his father that he loved his daughter very much, he never gave his grandson a father's mind, not humanity, where nowadays there is a lot of work to be seen. Diya was told that still humanity is alive somewhere because no one will probably know that foot aunt Maria had married her feet, their marriage did not last long because when Adrika came to her aunt, her husband Joseph Emmanuel Used to hate him a lot, there is also a secret behind this which is directly related to Adrika's father's feet, I neither know the secret behind it, nor did she ever reveal it, that's why Maria aunt gave her a relationship with him because she gave him enough time. He used to die too and many times he tried to kill Adrika too, not for himself but for someone else. A aunt Maria knew this very well so she always kept Adrika safe.

"*The pain was painful too*"

Feet say that the thing which we protect as much as we protect, that thing goes as far away from us, if something is going to happen in the world, then it will be there because neither one can China its fate, nor can anyone with its luck. And the other can join, this is such a waste that every person is aware of the thought of it, it is not necessary that when the nature of a person changes with time, then his thinking also shows a different picture at the same time, in the world a person from you Even though the legs may be bad, his thinking can never be far from him, because children die in the world, they don't think Joseph used to hate Adrika a lot in the past. Even more was that Bash used to tell her to separate him from Maria in any way, told him to hurt her so much that Maria could never see her and she also tried many times, every time Maria saved her .As the shadow of time began to move forward, Adrika also began to grow up for a while, now Joseph's evil eye was much more than her and Maria. It was wrong, it is said that even if someone's waste changes its path, the foot never changes its destination because it is not one's own, nor anyone's relationship is afraid, just like Adrika's life, even if it is wasted. The feet had changed, the floor was still the same Joseph had gone away from the dead and Adrika was far away from her feet, she was going to come back very soon, Maria knew this, so she took Adrika from Bangalore to a place where Joseph's Even the shadows could not follow her. Both Maria Uat and Adrika after all went to live in Goa, where Joseph's thinking was not even present at the time. Adrika was now a full 21 years old when she left Bangalore. Tak is worth the feet, the way the value of age increases, a person starts to consider himself better. Had kept it from everyone's evil eyes, now she was probably going to hit him because the way Adrika had seen her childhood, it seemed to her that she was out of her feet. Shiva is nothing more than a feast, because in those 6 years even though Joseph had gone away from her feet, after that Maria had faced many more surgery problems, so I thought that I should not make my Aunt Maria foot feast. And separating from them, let them also live their lives.

"Witness unknown

He played the feet of love"

One day Aadrika might have thought that now she would go away from her Aunt Maria, where would she say Ajaygi and how: she would say that she did not even know her herself and if she had said, how would she say that even though she had not brought him up and Even though she was not his real mother, the relationship that he had with Adrika could have been handled by someone else. After he broke down, he thought a lot that how should I say to Aunt Maria that I can't feast on him anymore because even though the pain was my feet, Aunt Maria has endured every one of his training with me when my Everyone had left together, then they raised me in the shadow of love, no matter how mean a person may be, he never forgets his feed, neither forgets his pain nor can he ever forget his love because He knows that what he was in the past is still there, so how could Adrika have changed and Kasah could have been away from her Aunt Maria? So he thought that after some more time, he would tell him the things that he just thought, because apparently the right thing is not to break his heart and not to cheat him in return, so he thought for a while. A little more time will pass then I will try to separate from Aunt Maria, after all there are some secrets that were going to come in her life like Adrika's father who was away from her, feet were always with her as well as a shadow By becoming who Adrika did not have malls that mother used to belong to a very big family and why her father did not belong to a big family like her mother, I mean because of the financial situation, Adrika's grandfather was a very big business, V Adrika's Father used to belong to a middle class family, foot Adrika's mother used to be infatuated with him, so he had told his father that if I would marry then I would do it only with Vikrant which was the name of Adrika's father, hence Adriek's grandfather was new. Didn't say anything for some time and got both of them married. Legs are after marriage. Shri Adrika's dad ji chal base that too because of heart attack.

III

The Strange Secret

There are some moments in life from which we always say to be distant, feet may not work all the time, because everyone in the world has trouble, feet do not mean that we should stop living because if we have got life then it means to live. And if you don't get it, then also think that you are the greatest person in the world who has passed every handwriting of pain and is lonely, it is never a problem to be alone that you are weak because never Sometimes it also means that you do not need anyone else and those who have many logs should be strong. Still, we try that this ritual is not met in our luck. That's why he left not only his house but also his family for the sake of Adrika, time took both of them. Had silenced the legs not weak, both of them even though they were away from their home, their feet were with each other, they always used to be happy whenever Adrika weak party aunt Maria supported her, she can never forget these batis and so many surgery memories That's why she had thought that there is no one else for aunt Maria except me Those times they say that when everything is going well in your life, only then someone comes into your world to trouble you in your gathering and at the same time a witness from their past knocks to give trouble to Adrika and Aunt Maria. The name of the trouble was none other than Adrika's father. Maria was present only at that time, so he first asked her where Adrika said, she had hurt her father. Time didn't say anything because she knew that the witness because of which Adrika lost her mother and also the male love that was about to meet her mother could not take her away because Adrika even though her Daughter was foot in her sorrow and pain, Aunt Maria always supported her, that's why she didn't say that someone else's bad shadow was also on her feet, so Aunt Maria told Adrika's father that she is in Hasotel now, she is not with me. Still, Adrika's father was not here at this time and I was not there because when Adrika's grandfather died in childhood, he had given his entire property in the name of his daughter and when Adrika's mother died. Before death, he had given his former property to Adrika and in the will paper, he had given his entire property to his daughter, in it it was clearly written that when Adrika turns 21, then she will give her property to anyone. It can give, it can keep itself, it can also donate and this thing Adrika's father was fully aware of and counted. Even so, he asked Adrika's father Vikrant to leave her, and he said that he would not leave until he met his daughter. Vikrant Rathore knew very well that as long as Maria is alive, she never sent Adrika with her and neither did Adrika That's why he would ever be able to get the property, so he asked to add to his son, which used to be his own, I mean from Joseph to Joseph, even though Aunt Maria had saved Adrika for a while, it was probably something else. Because at the time, both Vikrant Rathore together were going to do some such enmity, due to which the distance was going to come between Adrika and Aunt Maria, now these are cash distances, only after some time we all know the sky.

**"It is said that all was well
but someone's deceit took away our world from
us,
in whose shadow we were able to entertain
ourselves."**

Even though those days went away from her, there was a request to return soon, so Aunt Maria had thought that she would take Adrika away from her too, so she packed her own clothes and Adrika's clothes. Liya and got ready to go and in the same time Adrika would also come and when she sees the condition of the house, she asks her Aunt Mary that we are going where Mother Adrika called her mother for the first time. Was called tax and she could not even leave her happiness because the one who was going to leave the shadow of pain, she could not leave the happiness of life in her thinking, that's why she said that I was enough for you and not we are living in california Come on, my princess, so let's go, we both come walking around, why is there a problem, mother, nothing It is my princess, so take this a gift from my side. Said that her past was no longer going to leave her behind, the aunt was very worried because at the time of listening, when both of them were leaving her, then she saw Joseph's feet in front of Adrika, they did not even reveal that Joseph and Vikrant are chasing them both, so she took him to the airport sooner than him and told him that you go ahead, I will come in a while, till this Adrika also asked him what happened mother, why are you so upset So he said nothing bash, he is going to come to Chandu nor airport, he has to give him the keys of his shop, so I come by paying more. Aunt Maria had an airport in the distance of the place where she lived, so both of them went to the pouch very soon, that too half an hour before the time of catching the flight, they did this why the only reason behind this was both Joseph and Vikarnat of the time When Aunt Mary and Adrika were chasing they went to the pouch, when they both came in, then Aunt Maria Sir F was in front of them because they could not find both the pouches with Adrika, Aunt Maria had told Aadrika that the flight was half an hour late. Adrika had already sat down. And she didn't even know that Aunt Maria had just got her ticket cut, not hers because if Joseph and Vikrant had seen both of them together at the same time, Adrika would again go through the same pain and suffer. which she has already suffered in her past, if both of them had hated time, if she had taken the time, maybe her condition would have worsened, both of them could have killed her, so Aunt Mary made this plan in advance. Had taken that too to be safe and at happy time Aunt Maria had given her such a drink and said that as soon as she goes inside the flight, I come after a while to drink it, Adrika did not know that she had a drink. She would faint as soon as she drank it, and she would be far from her Aunt Maria. After all, when she met Vikrant and Joseph and when they asked her where Adrika was So he told them clearly that's why they both took him with them and what did they do with them after that you will know in the next chapter only .

> *"Worrying it was a matter of protection*
> *and some logs were walking with their feet,*
> *their souls was against me."*

It is said that there are some relationships in the world as well, whose truth we are very difficult to understand, that means we only ever know their true birth, what they tell us, those who care, they care, will we ever be able to do that like them? Life teaches us something new all the time, instead of learning it, we reject it, every moment bash thinks that what is right for us, it is wrong. The only pecan of the world that is with you is what you have. never leave mats with him because the superior is also watching your every single thing silently acquainting with each one he never left you alone he bash with you he is waiting when you move on in your life.

"Evening Even if it's down
Let's hope
We Still alive."

IV

The Pain Of Soul

We can bear every pain in life, we can never bear the
pain of being separated from someone, because at the time
we are not only separated from the human witness but

also from our own memories, which we have spent with him, with the one who Hard ki talim baati hai, how we will eradicate it, we don't get that birth, we don't have that much power that we can get away in two moments from what we know for many years, time seems to be silence is a patient party, someone else's support to move forward Take it, then and somewhere we can forget the human testimony, even then somewhere their friends stay with us, that locality, that house, those walls, all those memories of them remind us that we can not leave them, only People's hearts are not broken in love, but many people forget themselves even while playing the relationship, and in that many souls even try to forget their own pain. Which was about to happen with Adrika now. On this day Aunt Maria saved her. On this day, he sent Adrika to California by any means, the feet could not go at that time because if both of them would have been in the hands of both of them together at the same time, then both of them could have died at the same time, so Aunt Marian said this The plan was made long back when he saw Vikrant and Joseph together for the first time, so he had thought that whatever happens to me, nothing happens to Adrika in her feet by saving Emery Princess. After all, when he gave Adrika a drink and made her sit on the flight, then she was going back and at that time Joseph and Vikrant came and asked them to abduct them from the airport because when they asked about Adrika, they They did not tell anything about her at that time, so they thought that by kidnapping her, we would be able to cheat Adrika by any means, this would have been possible if she would tell them something, after that both Joseph and Vikrant together took her to Bangalore. He went to where his whole story began in Attet when he told him that When he took the feet, he asked him the address of Adrika a lot, feet every time he said that even if you take my life, even then I will not tell the address of Adrika, why do not you do anything? Then at that time he also said That we also see how her address: It has been a long time that Adrika and Aunt Maria were separated from each other, neither Adrika knew anything about Aunt Maria nor Adrika knew anything about them because Adrika This day not only california pauchi undefined so finally she went where she said that only two witnesses could lift the curtain from rahsehaya sh time one aunt maria whose condition was not at all good because those don used to give her a lot of trouble every day she used to give a new kiss He used to give so much trouble to them that he should tell Adrika's address by any means, he suffered for almost a month and did not tell anything about Adrika to both of them and Adrika also did not make any contact for that number of days, she had said Did not know that except for Aunt Maria, Bash knew that where Adrika was and In what condition is it. After all, a lot of time had passed, so Vikrant and Joseph also thought that there is no use in keeping it alive now, we should dig its grave in the school, meaning it should be murdered. Can't calculate feet, that night was probably a night of suffering for Adrika and Aunt Maria because they were both distant from each other. The love that was between those don's, may not be seen anywhere in the world, some relationships are made absolutely above all, this day was proved because even though Aunt Maria did not give birth to her with her own stomach, neither She was brought up in her house by keeping her for 9 months, yet she performed the duty of being a mother and respected her that she even gave her life in the end. It is also a matter of mystery that it was not only Vikrant and Joseph, but there were also two logs, which Vikrant could not even mention. Never did it in front of anyone, nor Joseph, when she was living her last conspiracies, because her legs had been stabbed thirty times with a knife, until it reached both her eyes I was taking the name of Adrika, even then both of them had buried her in the Rathore villa at the same time and made her samadhi in a room where she could not even hear anyone's voice, even when both of them had buried her feet. She was alive at that time and was taking her last instruments, after all, both Vikranta and Joseph, she left and Rathore Villa was closed for some time. Some have come to know and have said Vikarnat and Joseph and who were those two witnesses with them, it is still a secret undefined Is it really the hand of Vikarnat behind the death of Adrika's mother undefined Is it really that of Adrika's grandfather Death was caused by a heart attack that her mother was actually in a car accident undefined Did Adrika ever return to Bangalore undefined And Adrika said what Did she ever try to find aunt maria undefined Is aunt maria's spirit still wandering in the quest of her daughter in a rathore villa undefined and if adrika mehfooz is also there then where is the shish time? Did aunt maria say to her and not send her to a safe place undefined and when adrika would have competed then wouldn't she have asked who aunt maria is undefined and does adrika know that aunt maria is no longer in the world is.

"I have buried my soul for you.
Even today, my soul is in your lap:
my last mother-in-law."

This story is not over yet, but it has only just begun. Now the legend of revenge is also buoyed and the words of giving pain to the pain that anger has endured every single day are still undefined.

> *"The saying of the grave has been realized my*
> *enemies defeated for me.*
> *their poweris not even strong yet*
> *which can bury my anger in a crowded*
> *gathering."*

Happy Christmas Day

Merry Christmas

"Wishing you a season that's merry and bright with the light of God's love. Nothing ever seems too bad, too hard, or too sad when you've got a Christmas tree in the living room."

May this season be full of light and laughter for you and your family.

Greetings By:- **Sumeet Kumar**